Bear with Me written by David Michael Slater and illustrated by Davilyn Lynch

ISBN 978-1-60537-608-0

This book was printed in November 2021 at Nikara, M. R. Štefánika 858/25, 963 01 Krupina, Slovakia.

First Edition
10 9 8 7 6 5 4 3 2 1

Clavis Publishing supports the First Amendment and celebrates the right to read.

Written by David Michael Slater
Illustrated by Davilyn Lynch

BEAR *with* ME

FIRST DAY
OF SCHOOL

Clavis

NEW YORK

"You sure you need to take Mr. Kalamazoo
with you?" Max's mom asked.
"For protection," Max told her.
"Don't worry, I won't let him eat anyone."
"Oh, sweetie," his mom said.
"I think you'll be *tickled pink* today!"

"KEEP AWAY!"

Max warned everyone on the bus.
"Wild animal up in here!
He gets nervous around strangers.
And he gets hungry when he's nervous!"

"GRRR,"
growled Mr. Kalamazoo.

Homeroom didn't go as well. Mr. Kalamazoo got nervous and wouldn't let Max introduce himself to his new classmates.

At least he didn't eat anyone.

And lunch was even worse.
Mr. Kalamazoo went
totally BERSERK.

"I TOLD YOU HE GETS HUNGRY WHEN HE'S NERVOUS!"

Max cried. "It's not my fault he's a sloppy eater!"

That's how Max and Mr. Kalamazoo ended up
in Mrs. Gingerbread's office. She called Max's mom
to come get him . . . right away.

Max and Mr. Kalamazoo were sent to wait on the blue bench.
That's when a girl with a pink backpack walked over
and sat down next to them.
"WATCH OUT," Max warned her.
"Mr. Kalamazoo is dangerous!"
"So is Fluffmeistergeneral," said the girl.
"Who?" Max asked.

The girl opened her backpack,
and out climbed a giant pink polar bear with a pink bow in her fur.
Mr. Kalamazoo growled at Fluffmeistergeneral.

But then Fluffmeistergeneral put her paws on Mr. Kalamazoo's shoulders and said, "Don't worry. It gets better every day. We got sent home our first day too. I may or may not have tried to hibernate in my cubby."

Then Fluffmeistergeneral *hugged* Mr. Kalamazoo.
And Mr. Kalamazoo *hugged* Fluffmeistergeneral back.

"See ya tomorrow," Fluffmeistergeneral said.
"See ya tomorrow," Mr. Kalamazoo said back.
Then they both climbed into their backpacks.

"Madi," said the girl with the pink backpack.
She held out her hand to Max. "I'm *tickled pink* to meet you."
"Max," said Max, putting out his hand. "I'm *tickled pink* to meet you, too."
They shook hands.

"Well," said Max's mom.
"You made it
through most
of the day."
"Barely," said Max.